My Whirling, Twirling Motor

For Sabrina, Maclean, and Tabitha. My endless list of wonderful—MS

For my mom, who always pointed out everything I did right.
Thank you for allowing me to make my dreams come true—TL

American Psychological Association
750 First Street NE
Washington, DC 20002

Magination Press is a registered trademark of the American Psychological Association.
Order books here: maginationpress.org or 1-800-374-2721

Book design by Susan White
Printed by Worzalla, Stevens Point, WI

Library of Congress Cataloging-in-Publication Data
Names: Saunders, Merriam Sarcia, author. | Lyon, Tammie, illustrator.
Title: My whirling, twirling motor / by Merriam Sarcia Saunders ; illustrated by Tammie Lyon.
Description: Washington, DC : Magination Press, [2019] | American Psychological Association.
Summary: A young boy with ADHD feels like he is constantly driven by a 'motor.'
He is constantly getting in trouble, even when he is not trying to be naughty.
But his mom helps him focus on the things he does right each day —
Provided by publisher.
Identifiers: LCCN 2018040691| ISBN 9781433829369 (hardcover)
| ISBN 1433829363 (hardcover)
Subjects: |CYAC: Attention-deficit hyperactivity
disorder—Fiction.
Classification: LCC PZ7.1.S269 My 2019 | DDC [E]—dc23
LC record available at https://lccn.loc.gov/2018040691

Manufactured in the United States of America
10 9 8 7 6 5 4 3 2 1

My Whirling, Twirling Motor

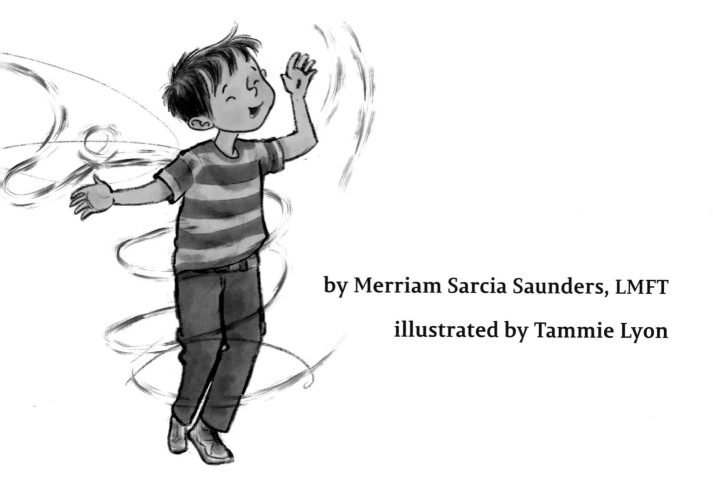

by Merriam Sarcia Saunders, LMFT

illustrated by Tammie Lyon

MAGINATION PRESS · WASHINGTON, DC
American Psychological Association

I have a spinning motor inside me
that buzzes and whirls and hums.
I can't turn it off. It made me play
with my dinosaurs instead of
getting my shoes on this morning.

At school, my motor made me wiggle
too much during story time.

I touched the teacher's scissors.

And I talked out of turn.

Whirling, spinning, humming.

At recess, my friends wouldn't play with me because my buzzing motor's noises were too annoying.

So I threw a ball hard and hit Nicole in the face. By mistake. Ouch. Sorry Nicole.

The twirling and humming
made me forget my snack.

And my lunch.

And my homework.

At home, the motor ran me
fast around the dining table.
Running and running and
running. Round and round.

Mom told me to slow down, take it easy.
But I couldn't turn off the motor.

So Dad had me sit down
and he plunked a box of
blocks in front of me.

Up, up, and up, I kept going.
Higher and higher.

I made a tower. So high
it almost hit the ceiling.

Charlie!
Dinner
NOW!

Mom and Dad
came to get me.
They had mad faces.

Now it's time for bed.
Dad chases me twice around the sofa.

Mom tells me to
brush my teeth.

But I can't sleep. I have a spinning motor
inside me that buzzes and whirls and hums.

Mom tucks me in and I squiggle and squirm because the motor is busy.

Hey there, wiggle worm. I know it's hard for you to settle down. You always move, move, move! But I need to talk to you.

Uh oh. Will she tell me all the things
I did because of my buzzing motor?

I bury my head under a blanket.

I wish I could turn off the motor!

She takes out a sparkly red
notebook and reads from a list.

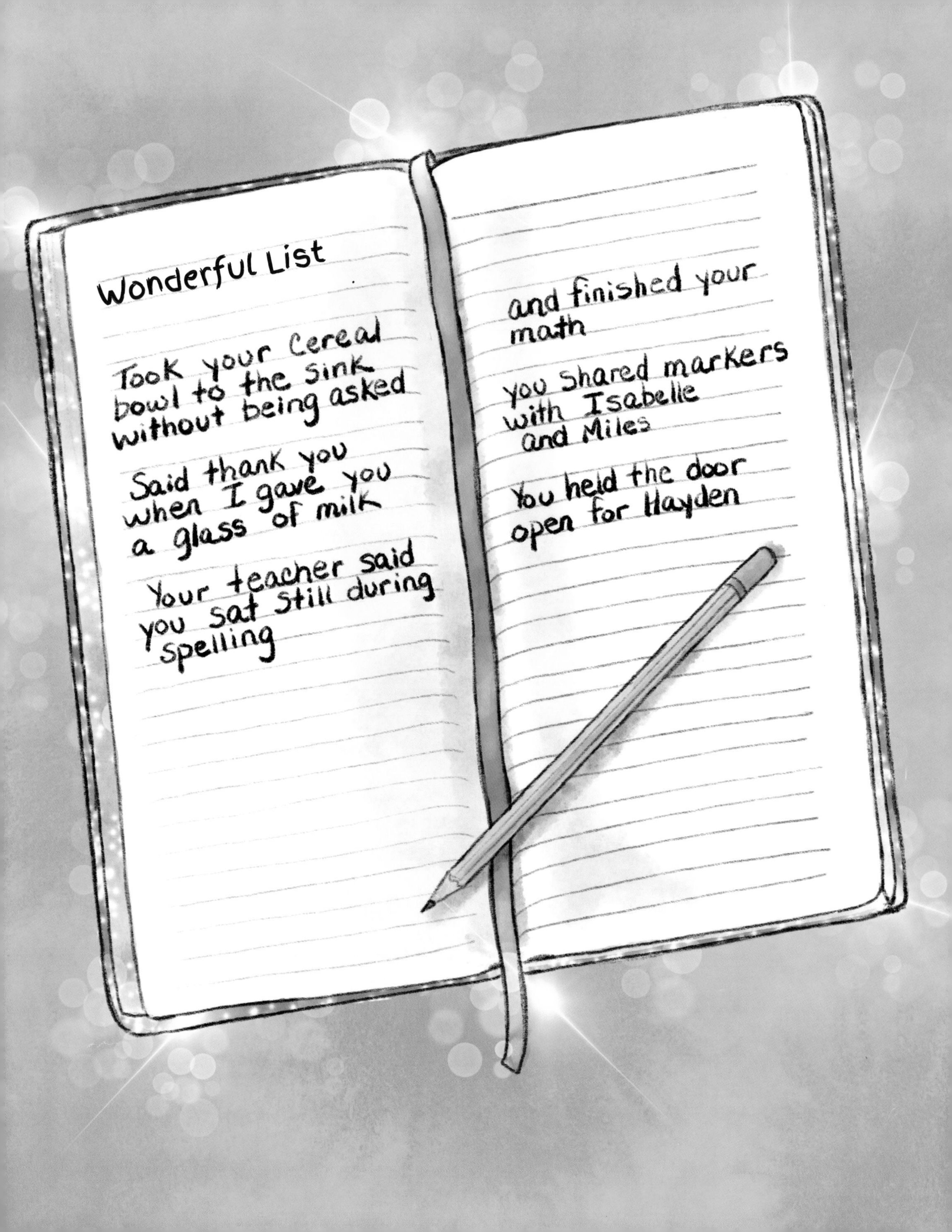

Wonderful List

Took your cereal
bowl to the sink
without being asked

Said thank you
when I gave you
a glass of milk

Your teacher said
you sat still during
spelling

and finished your
math

You shared markers
with Isabelle
and Miles

You held the door
open for Hayden

"You ate all your peas. And broccoli.

And you put your blocks away.

You got into your jammies for Dad much quicker today.

You brushed your teeth the first time I told you to.

...and I'm very proud of you."

My buzzing, twirling, humming motor settles to a quiet purr. And a warm, cozy, yumminess spreads.

I like this feeling.

Mom ruffles my hair. "You did all that today! I wrote it all down to remind us all how wonderful you are. I bet I'll catch you doing all sorts of wonderful things tomorrow, too."

I dig down into my warm covers.
I guess my motor is a little sleepy after all.

Good night.

Dad says "Good night."
Mom kisses my forehead.
They think I'm wonderful.

What will be on my Wonderful List tomorrow?

Note to Parents, Caregivers, & Teachers

"A person who feels appreciated will always do more than expected."
—Author unknown

Lots of children feel as though they have a constantly spinning motor inside, which sometimes causes them to be restless and impulsive. This is especially true for children with AD/HD or similar executive-functioning disorders (in fact, front and center in the Diagnostic and Statistical Manual's criteria for AD/HD is the symptom of acting as if "driven by a motor"!), but can be true for any child with excess energy. Being unable to sit still, being restless, and being difficult to keep up with are common issues. At the end of a long day, it's easy for adults to focus on all the trouble these "motor-driven" behaviors have caused.

Studies have shown that the most effective way to reduce an unwanted behavior or increase a desired one is by using a repeated and consistent consequence. Consequences, despite the common association with the term, are not just negative! A consequence, technically, is anything that happens as a result of an action, and can be either pleasant, in the form of a reward, or not so enjoyable, in the form of punishment. Most children don't set out to behave in reckless and impulsive ways. Getting reprimanded for behavior that was unintentional can often lead to feelings of shame, uncertainty, and a lack of self-esteem. Simply put, punishment leaves our kids feeling badly about what they did unintentionally and does little to aid them in doing better next time. If you reflect on the teachers and bosses you've had over the years, which ones motivated you to work hard, stay late, and do your best? Was it the ornery boss and the authoritarian teacher who pointed out your flaws? Or the encouraging, forgiving one who praised your work?

But how do we reward a child who is just so gosh darn difficult all the time? Sometimes it is exhausting just keeping up with them, making sure they behave appropriately in class, learn to clean up, sit still, and don't act out. It takes practice on our part, as well, but there are plenty of things we can do to encourage appropriate behavior!

Notice them "doing good."
Start with a certain behavior you wish to reduce, and allow yourself to ignore most other frustrating behaviors (provided it is safe to do so—of course, hitting, biting, running away, etc. need to be immediately addressed). Now, identify the opposite of the behavior. For example, if your child frequently interrupts, then your task is to look for the times your child doesn't interrupt, point it out immediately, and reward it.

Give rewards.
We often associate the word reward with material things, but that doesn't have to be the case. Rewards can also come in the form of privileges (TV or video game time, a story read aloud, a game with a parent). And one of the highest forms of rewards for our children is praise! Goodness knows that an impulsive child probably gets reprimanded far more frequently than praised, so words of

encouragement and thanks are like gold. If you use a point or token system that leads to a material reward, the reward should come fairly quickly, or the connection between good behavior and the positive result is lost. The reward should be desirable enough to motivate your child to do the hard work. And, because boredom is a big foe of hyperactive children, the reward should be frequently changed so the novelty of your system doesn't fade.

Be consistent.

Try this consistently for a week. You may be surprised to see how your child begins to gear their behavior towards the type that earns praise. During the first week, if they misstep, try to ignore it. Later, you can address it by lightheartedly saying, "Darn, looks like you're having a hard time with not interrupting right now. But sometimes you're really good at it! I bet you'll get it next time."

Choose your battles.

Unfortunately, sometimes whirling, twirling motors cause kids to act out in ways that hurt themselves or others, and obviously that cannot be ignored. An adult needs to step in to stop the behavior, without shaming the child, and to provide a pause and a teachable moment. Many times during an acting-out behavior, the child's brain is on overdrive and can't think logically or regulate emotions. Now is not the time to address the behavior! Providing a pause in the form of a space to calm down and reflect (the child's room or a quiet place alone) may be just the thing they need. It doesn't help to frame this as a time-out or punishment, as likely the behavior was impulsive and unintentional, and they may have even shocked themselves. After they're calm, reflect on what you saw, what you

imagine they felt, and how they can handle it differently in the future. "I don't think you meant to yell at your sister, you must have been really angry. What are some better ways to handle anger if that happens again?" Providing alternatives in the form of words to express anger, a journal they can draw or write in, or a pillow they can scream into can teach them better ways to cope. The goal is to create a mindfulness around the impulsivity, to teach them to learn to pause before acting, and to teach alternate behaviors. Having your child take ownership of the outcome is also important, and restorative justice is good for this. Without the need for shame, your child can help clean up the aftermath of his tantrum, apologize for yelling, scaring, or hurting, or write a note or draw a picture to make up for being rude. And don't forget praise for how proud you are that they took responsibility!

Start your own Wonderful List!

Once you are practiced at noticing one good behavior, you will start to see it all! Start your own Wonderful List! Let your child decorate the notebook, then keep it in a handy place and write down as many positives as you can catch. Did they pick up their socks? Write it down! Did they say please? Write it down! Drew a beautiful picture? It goes on the list! As they get older, their Wonderful List will be a thing to reflect on and cherish for the both of you.

Remind yourself!

In a busy day, it can be easy to forget to notice. Put sticky notes around the house to remind yourself to praise what your child is doing this very minute that pleases you and to put it on the list. You can also set reminders in your phone or establish routine times of day to check.

Let's face it—parenting a child with a whirling, twirling motor is not easy. It can be tiring and you are frequently frustrated and angry. After a week of noticing the good and praising, you will likely feel greater empathy and positive regard towards your child, because you are more focused on what they're doing right. And don't forget to praise yourself. Parents often either feel like failures, or are made to feel that way by others. You are doing better than you probably give yourself credit for.

At the end of the day, while you're taking your child's positive inventory, don't forget to appreciate yourself.

Our children do so many wonderful things all day! Reading the long list to them at bedtime will inspire them to earn your praise, feels gratifying for you, too, and, perhaps more importantly, will fill their often shallow self-esteem buckets to the brim where they belong.

About the Author

MERRIAM SARCIA SAUNDERS, LMFT, is a psychotherapist who has worked in private practice and as a school counselor, specializing in helping families of children with autism spectrum disorder, AD/HD, and learning disabilities. She writes picture books and novels for children that portray issues in a way that allows kids to see themselves, and others to understand. She lives in Northern California and has three kids and a dog. Visit @merriammft on Twitter and merriamsbooks.com.

About the Illustrator

TAMMIE LYON is the award-winning author and illustrator of numerous books for children. She is known for her work on the *Eloise* books as well as the wildly popular *Katie Woo* series. Tammie's first written and illustrated title, *Olive and Snowflake*, received starred reviews from both *Kirkus* and *School Library Journal*. She lives in Cincinnati, Ohio. Visit @tammielyon on Instagram and Twitter, and behance.net/tammielyon.

About Magination Press

MAGINATION PRESS is the children's book imprint of the American Psychological Association, the largest scientific and professional organization representing psychologists in the United States and the largest association of psychologists worldwide. Visit maginationpress.org